HENRY HECKELBECK

Takes a Swing

By **Wanda Coven**

Illustrated by **Priscilla Burris**

LITTLE SIMON

New York   Amsterdam/Antwerp   London   Toronto   Sydney   New Delhi

LITTLE SIMON

An imprint of Simon & Schuster Children's Publishing Division
1230 Avenue of the Americas, New York, New York 10020
First Little Simon hardcover edition January 2025
© 2025 by Simon & Schuster, LLC
Also available in a Little Simon paperback edition.
For information about special discounts for bulk purchases, please contact Simon & Schuster Special Sales at 1-866-506-1949 or business@simonandschuster.com. The Simon & Schuster Speakers Bureau can bring authors to your live event. For more information or to book an event contact the Simon & Schuster Speakers Bureau at 1-866-248-3049 or visit our website at www.simonspeakers.com.
Designed by Chrisila Maida
Manufactured in the United States of America 1224 LAK
10 9 8 7 6 5 4 3 2 1
Library of Congress Cataloging-in-Publication Data
Names: Coven, Wanda, author. | Burris, Priscilla, illustrator.
Title: Henry Heckelbeck takes a swing / by Wanda Coven ; illustrated by Priscilla Burris. Description: First Little Simon paperback edition. | New York : Little Simon, 2025. | Series: Henry Heckelbeck ; book 17 | Audience term: Children | Audience: Ages 5–9. | Summary: After joining the Brewster Batters, Henry discovers that playing baseball is harder than he thought.
Identifiers: LCCN 2024010753 (print) | LCCN 2024010754 (ebook) | ISBN 9781665962933 (paperback) | ISBN 9781665962940 (hardcover) | ISBN 9781665962957 (ebook)) | Subjects: CYAC: Baseball—Fiction. | Sportsmanship—Fiction. | Friendship—Fiction.) | Classification: LCC PZ7.C83393 Hqu 2025 (print) | LCC PZ7.C83393 (ebook) | DDC [Fic]—dc23
LC record available at https://lccn.loc.gov/2024010753
LC ebook record available at https://lccn.loc.gov/2024010754

CONTENTS

Chapter 1 NICE CATCH! 1

Chapter 2 SERIOUS BUSINESS 11

Chapter 3 ALL IN 21

Chapter 4 NO "T" IN BASEBALL 33

Chapter 5 FOUL BALL 45

Chapter 6 DOOMSVILLE 57

Chapter 7 TO BE A STAR 69

Chapter 8 LET THE GAME BEGIN 79

Chapter 9 HENRY IS UP! 89

Chapter 10 BUTT WHAT? 103

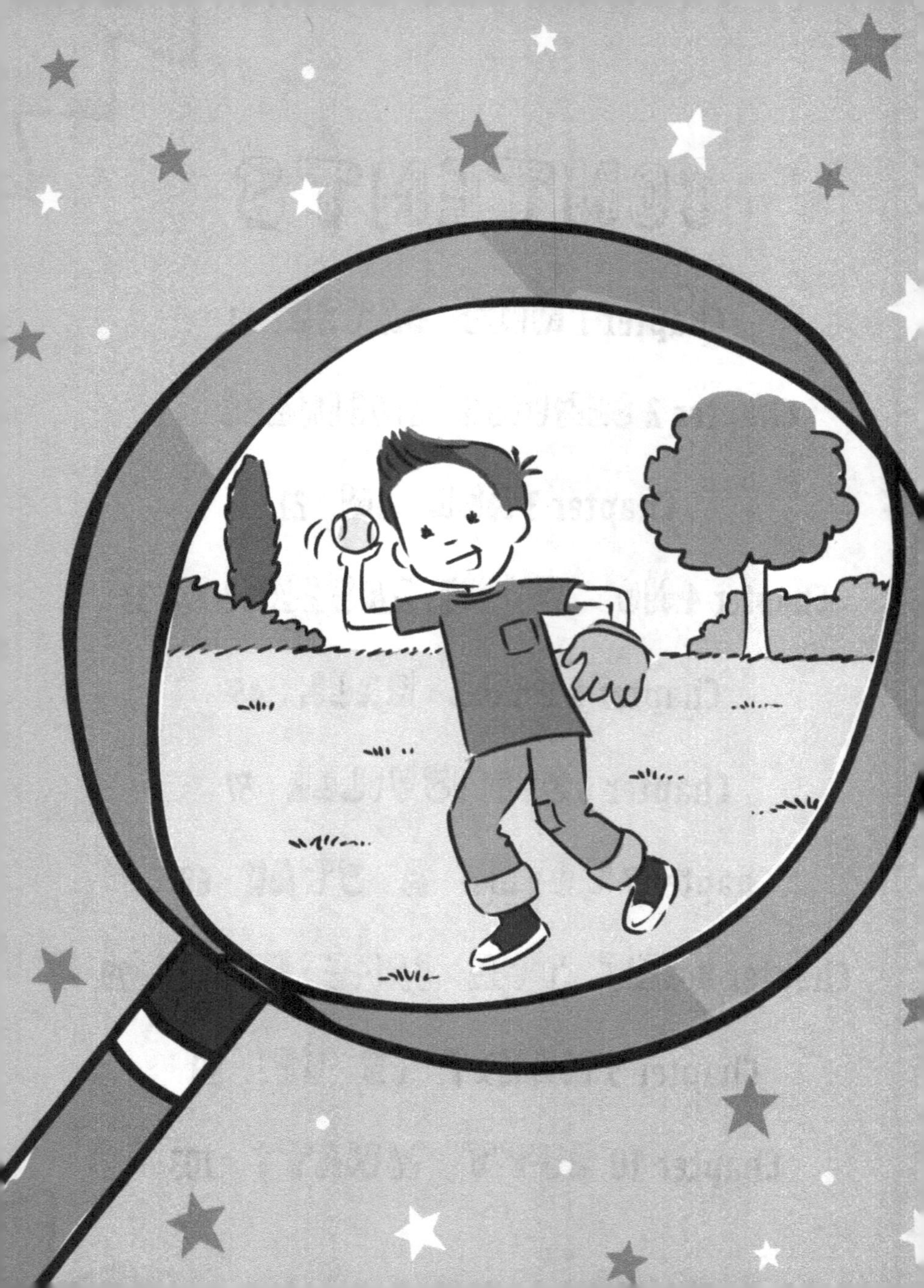

Chapter 1

NICE CATCH!

"READY?" Henry Heckelbeck called. He threw a baseball into the air.

Whap! Dudley Day caught it in his glove and took two steps back, away from Henry.

Dudley threw the ball to Max Maplethorpe, who sandwiched the ball in her glove. Then *she* took two steps back.

The three best friends were playing catch at the park.

Each time one of them caught the ball, they took two steps back.

Max threw to Henry. Henry slid across the grass with his glove wide open.

Plop! The ball fell right in, and his friends cheered.

"What a catch!" shouted Max.

"We're getting good at this!" Dudley agreed.

Henry got up and took two steps back. Now they were really far apart.

Henry gave the next ball a little too much power. The ball soared right over Dudley and rolled across the ground.

Sam Sterling caught the ball
and walked over.

Sam was one of their
classmates, and he was
wearing a baseball uniform.

"Are you joining the Brewster
Batters?" Sam asked.

He pointed to the baseball field on the other side of the park. "Our first practice starts in fifteen minutes."

"Not me," said Max. "I promised my mom I'd be home soon."

Henry and Dudley looked at each other.

"Well, *we* can!" said Henry.

The boys waved goodbye to Max and followed Sam to the baseball field.

Sam's baseball jersey had a big 8 and STERLING printed on the back.

Henry wanted a jersey with HECKELBECK printed on it.

Joining the baseball team was going to be a total blast!

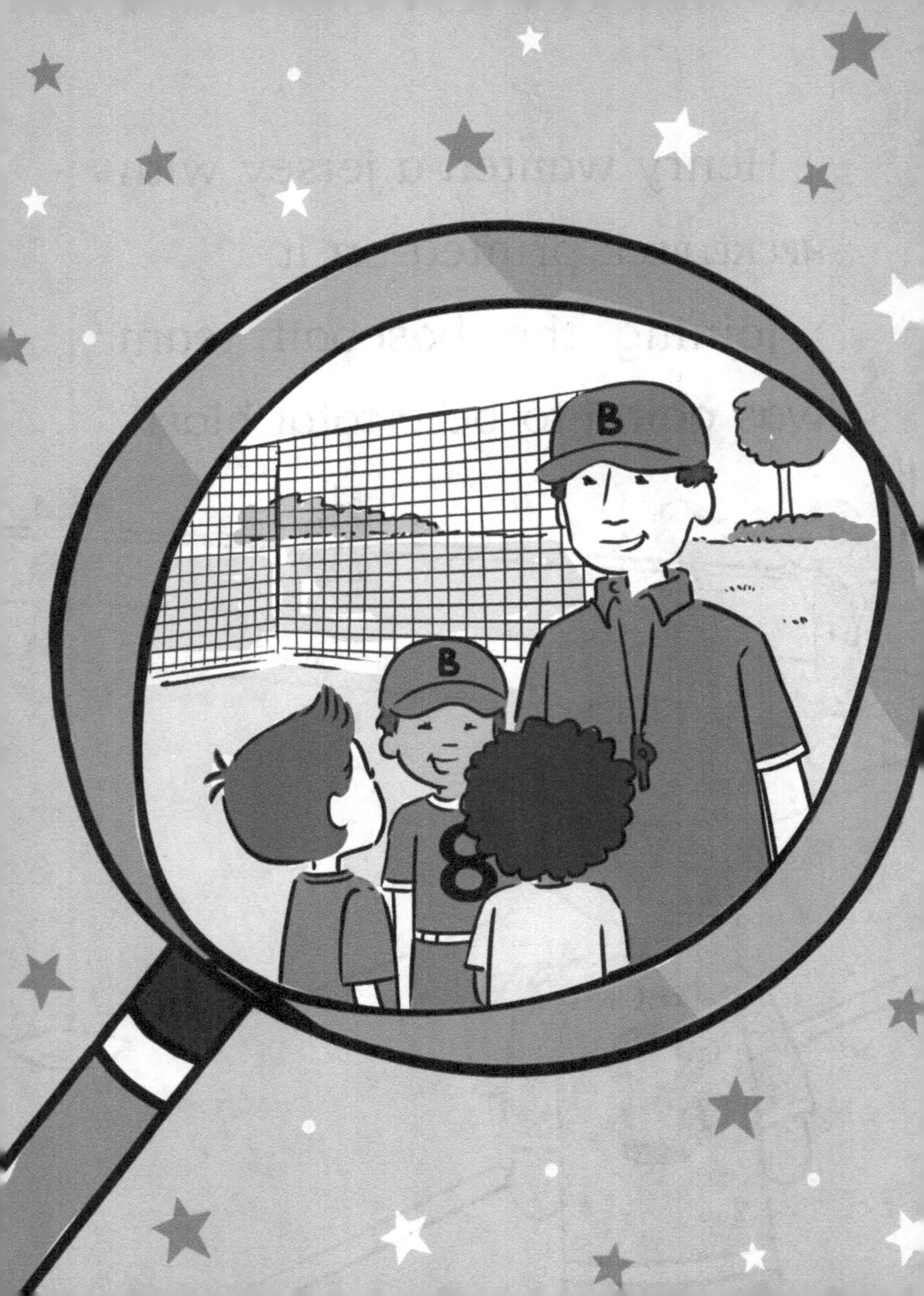

Chapter 2

SERIOUS BUSINESS

Sam introduced Henry and Dudley to Coach Hunt, the head of the Brewster Batters baseball team.

"Welcome!" said the coach. "You can practice with us."

"If you decide you want to officially join the team, your grown-ups need to fill out these papers," Coach Hunt explained.

Then Coach Hunt picked up a sack of baseballs and slung them over his shoulder. "Our first game is Thursday. You can turn in your papers after the game."

"Wow," Henry said. "A real game in two days!"

Coach Hunt chirped his whistle. Everyone began jogging around the baseball diamond. After they were finished running, they moved on to warm-up stretches.

"Circle those arms as BIG as
you can!" Coach Hunt called.

"This is hard work!" Dudley
said.

But Henry was used to these exercises from soccer. He circled his arms even faster.

"Time for some butt-kickers!" Coach Hunt said. He started running in place,

kicking his butt with the back
of his heel with every step.

Henry and Dudley joined in,
giggling. Then a boy turned
around to glare at them.

"Come on!" he said.
"Baseball is SERIOUS!"

When the boy turned away, Henry saw the last name LAWSON printed across the back of his jersey.

Henry and Dudley didn't like getting yelled at. They zipped their mouths shut for the rest of the warm-ups.

Zip! Zip!

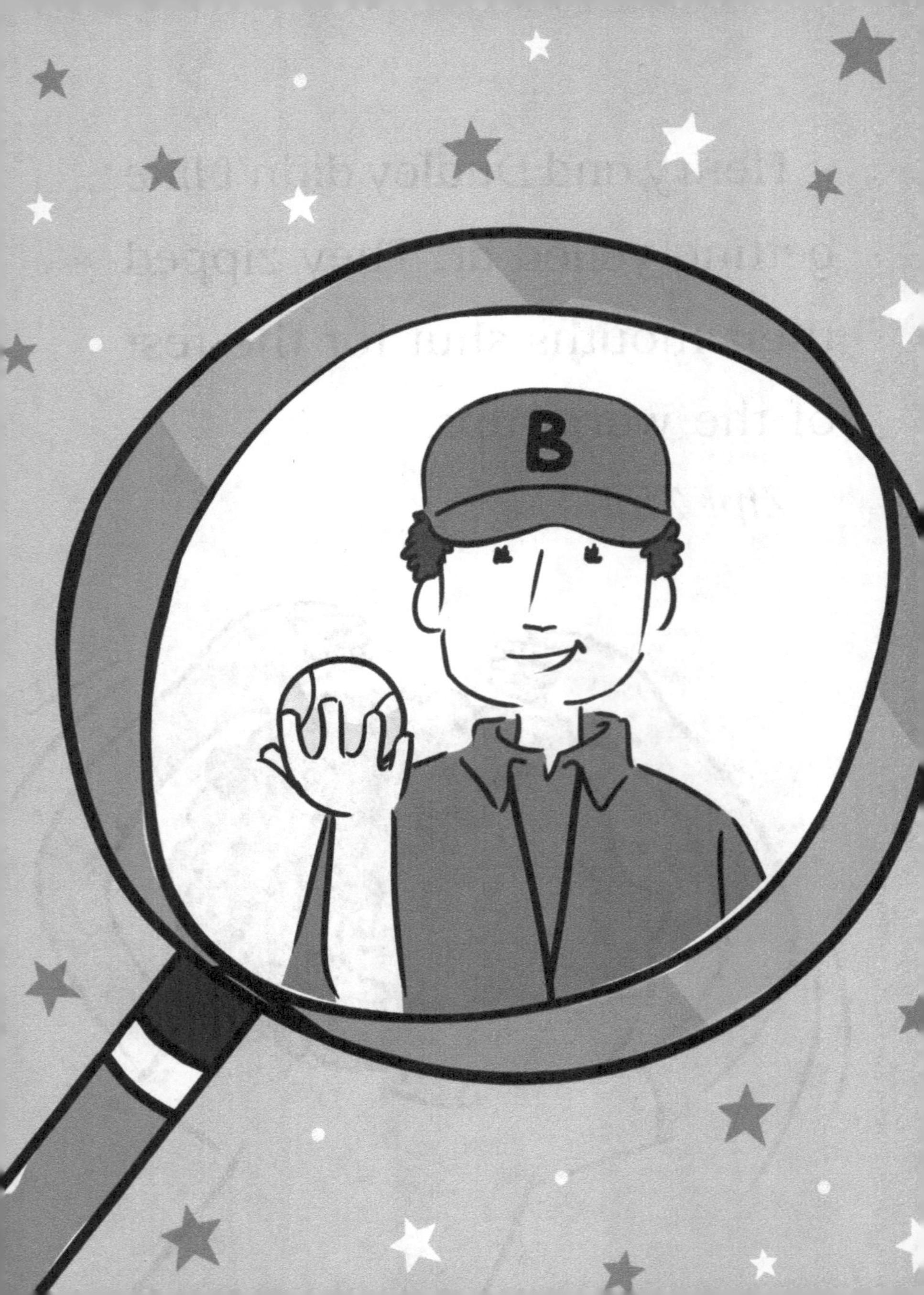

Chapter 3
ALL IN

"Now grab a ball and team up with a partner," Coach Hunt said. "We're going to practice throwing."

Henry and Dudley were partners, of course.

Dudley threw a high ball to
Henry. Henry tried to throw a
high ball back, but it wobbled
to the left.

"Point your toe at Dudley," Coach Hunt suggested. "At the same time you step forward, start your windup. As you let go of the ball, snap your wrist."

Henry tried to do what the coach suggested, but his whole body felt so stiff. When he threw the ball, it went straight into the ground!

Coach Hunt blew his whistle again. "Now, everybody, switch partners."

This time Henry got paired with Lucas Lawson—the boy who had yelled at him and Dudley.

Henry threw the ball to Lucas. The ball flew straight toward the ground again. But Lucas dropped his glove and caught it before it hit the ground.

"Wow, nice save!" Henry said.

Lucas shrugged like it was no big deal.

Lucas threw the ball hard and fast back to Henry. *Whack!*

Ow-eee! Henry thought. *That ball felt like it had rocket blasters on it!*

"Nice toss, Lucas!" Henry said, even though his hand stung like crazy. "You're really good at baseball!"

Lucas pinched the brim of his baseball cap.

"That's because I practice *every* day," he said. "If you don't practice, you won't get better.

If you don't get better, you won't go pro."

Henry eyes widened. *Go pro? Wow, that's serious,* he thought.

Henry wound up to throw the ball back. But this time, the ball slipped out of his hand and rolled behind him.

"Oops!" Henry said. As he turned around to pick up the ball, he heard Lucas sigh.

Geez, these Brewster Batters sure are serious about baseball, he thought. *They're . . . ALL IN!*

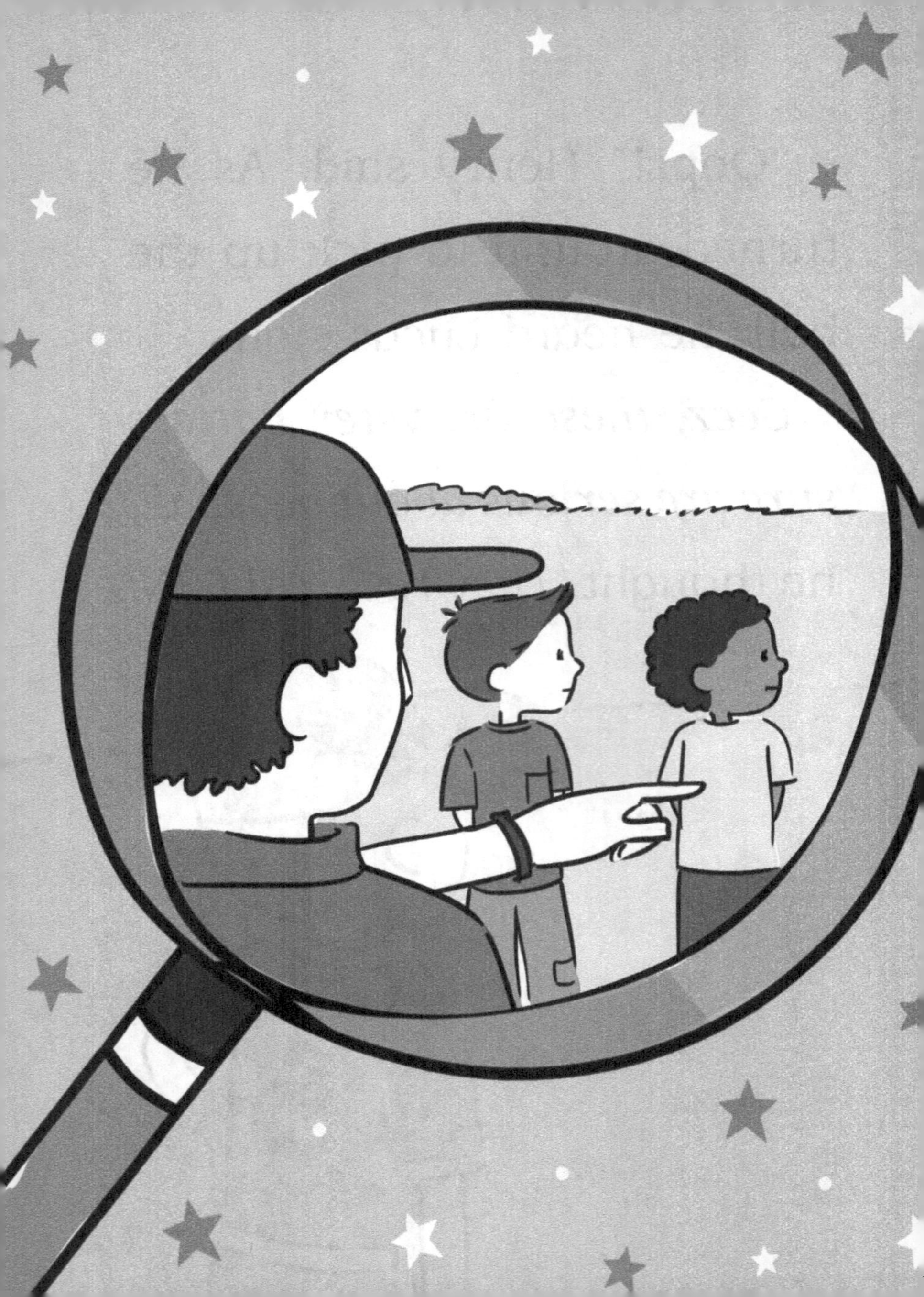

Chapter 4

NO "T" IN BASEBALL

Next Coach Hunt divided everyone into two teams. He also assigned each player a position.

Henry and Dudley both got assigned to right field.

Lucas was in charge of guarding third base. And Sam was on the other team.

"I've never played a real baseball game before," Henry told Dudley as they headed for the outfield.

"Me neither," Dudley said.

They turned around and faced home plate. From where they stood, it seemed miles away.

"Hey, where's the tee?" asked Dudley.

Henry squinted toward home plate. He watched as Coach Hunt pitched a ball from the pitcher's mound. The batter swung and missed.

Henry's jaw dropped.

"Dudley, there is no tee! You have to swing at a ball that's thrown at you!" Henry said.

"Whoa! This is the *real* deal," Dudley replied.

The boys were so stunned,
they didn't notice Coach Hunt
pitch the ball again.

Whack! The batter hit the
ball, and it flew straight toward
Henry and Dudley.

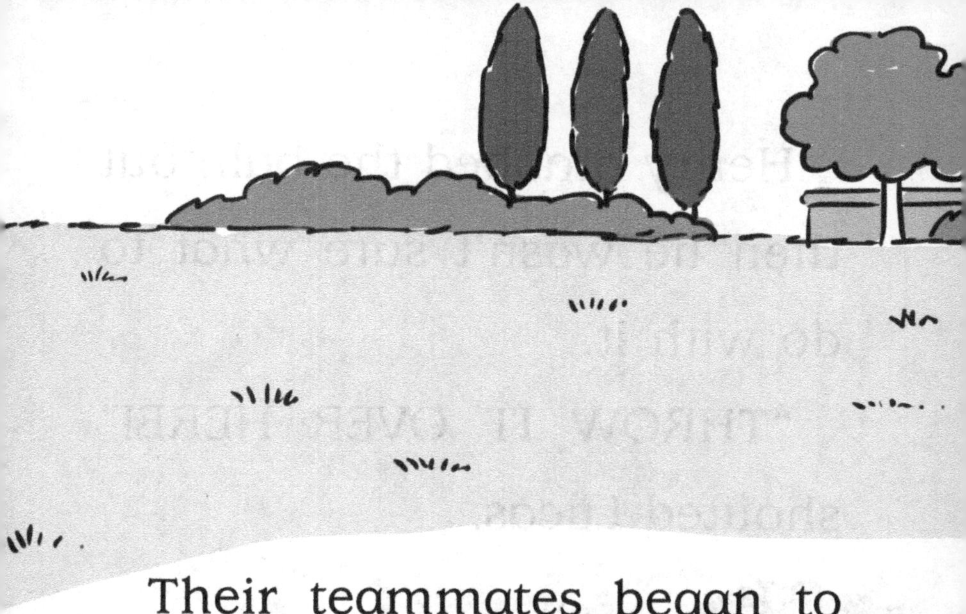

Their teammates began to shout.

Henry and Dudley went for the ball at the same time . . . and crashed into each other. The ball fell on the ground between them.

Henry grabbed the ball, but then he wasn't sure what to do with it.

"THROW IT OVER HERE!" shouted Lucas.

Henry threw the ball as hard as he could toward third base. Lucas caught it, but he was too late. The batter was safe on third.

Dudley nudged Henry and said, "Sorry for crashing into you. Are you okay?"

Henry wiped some grass off his pants.

"Yeah, I'm fine," he said. "But I blew that play."

And that didn't make Henry feel good at all.

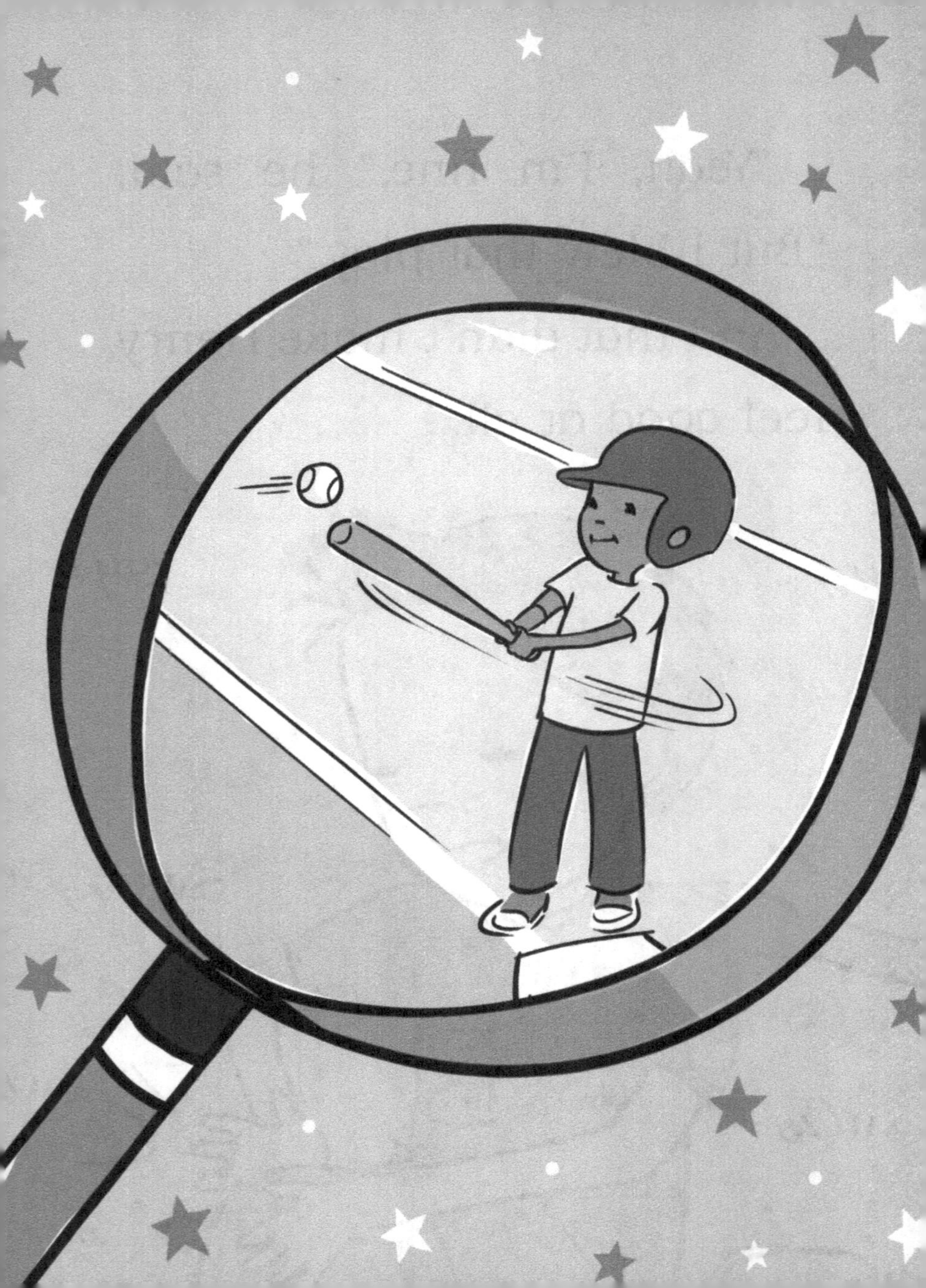

Chapter 5
FOUL BALL

When Henry's team went up to bat, Henry made sure he was last in line. But Dudley ended up first!

Coach Hunt pitched the ball. It zipped toward home plate.

Crack! Dudley hit it on his first try! Gripping the bat, he raced to first base.

"GOOOO, DUDLEY!" Henry yelled. Then he looked at his

teammates. Why was he the only one cheering?

Coach Hunt left the pitcher's mound and walked Dudley back to home plate.

"Your ball went over the line," Coach Hunt explained, tapping the line between home plate and first base. "It has to stay within the lines to be a fair ball."

Henry covered his mouth. Now he knew why no one else had cheered. Dudley had hit a foul ball!

"Also, next time, drop the bat before you run," Coach Hunt added. He tapped the bat, still gripped tightly in Dudley's hands.

Dudley let out a big sigh.
And if that wasn't enough, he
missed the next two swings
and struck out.

Before he knew it, it was
Henry's turn.

He slowly walked past all his teammates.

That's when he heard Lucas whisper, "You're not even on the team yet."

That just made Henry walk
even slower.

Ouch, he thought. *Why did
Lucas have to say THAT?*

Henry's knees shook as he
picked up the bat. Just then
a man walked onto the field.

He wore a shirt that said PLAY T-BALL!

"It's our turn to use the field," the man said.

"We only have one more batter," Coach Hunt replied, nodding toward Henry.

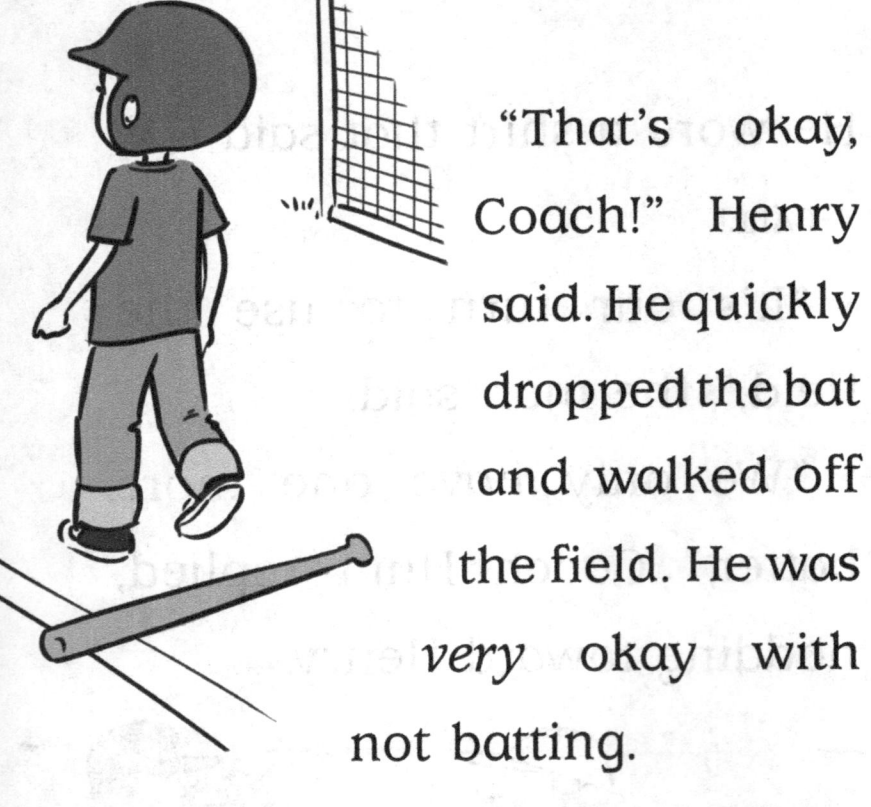

"That's okay, Coach!" Henry said. He quickly dropped the bat and walked off the field. He was *very* okay with not batting.

"Thanks for understanding, Heckelbeck," Coach Hunt said. "I'll make sure you bat at Thursday's game!"

Henry's shoulders tightened.

Oh great, he thought. *That means I'll bat for the first time in a REAL game. What if I flub up?*

Just the thought of it made Henry feel like he'd already struck out.

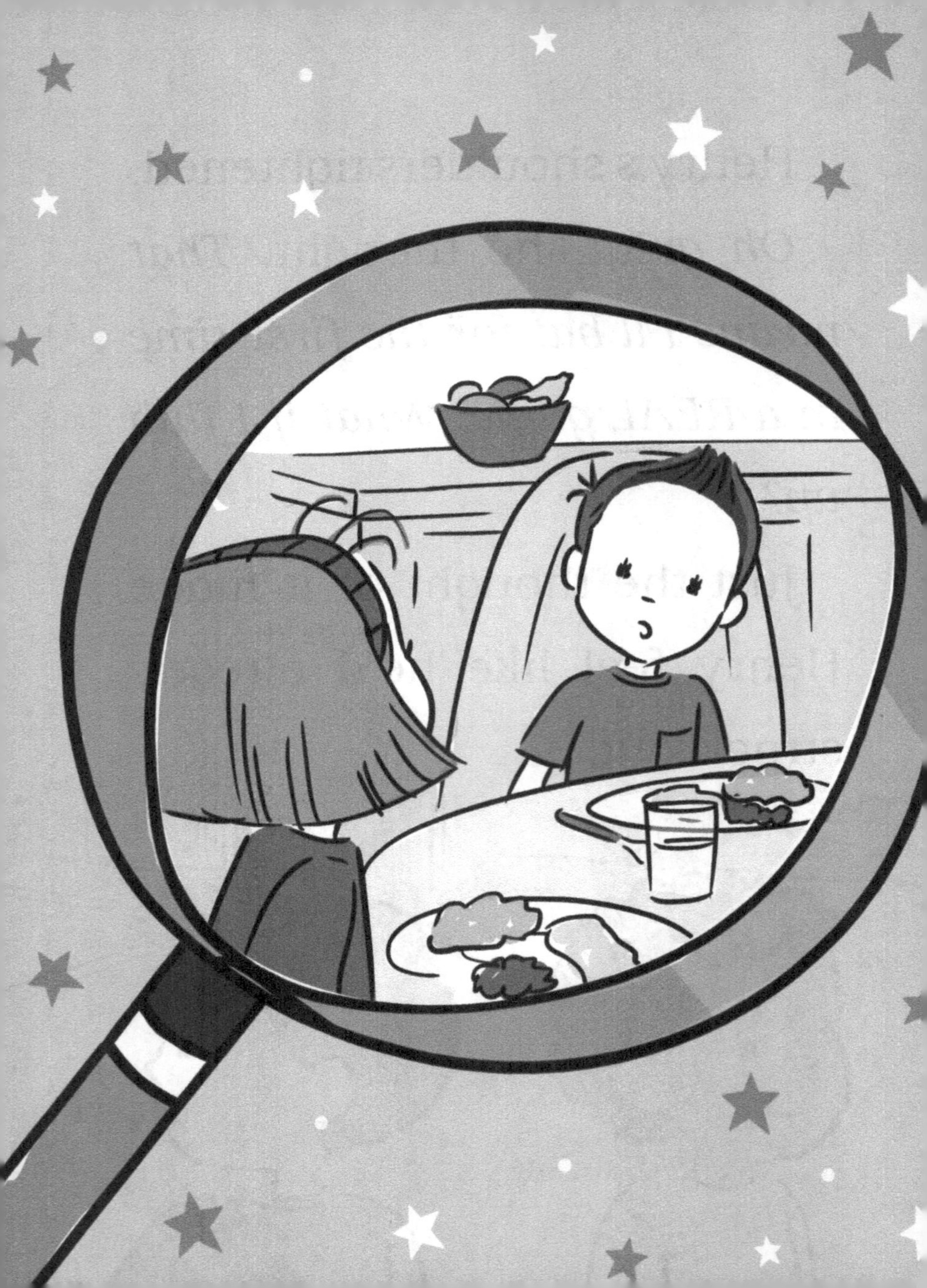

Chapter 6

DOOMSVILLE

At dinner Henry handed his parents the papers for joining the Brewster Batters.

"I'll go to your game on Thursday!" Heidi said.

"Really?" Henry asked.

"Yeah," Heidi replied. "I want to see my little brother hit a home run!"

Henry frowned. *Home run? I wish!*

After dinner Henry went to his room. He imagined striking out in front of his whole family . . . and he did *not* like that image.

He dropped a pillow onto the floor for home plate. Then he pulled a ruler out of his desk drawer.

Henry swung the ruler a few times, but he felt silly. *Like THIS is going to help!* he grumped to himself.

Flopping onto his bed, Henry
groaned. "I'm so doomed."

While Henry was in
Doomsville, something fell off
his shelf. *Thump!*

Henry rolled over to see what it was. And there, on the floor, sat his glowing magic book.

"Yay!" cried Henry.

Just like a baseball player dives for a ball, Henry dove for the book. He sat cross-legged on the floor as the book opened up to a spell.

Star Baseball Player

Are you worried about your first baseball game? Perhaps you need to be a better batter, thrower, and catcher? If you want to be a superstar player without putting in the work, then this is the spell for you!

Ingredients:
1 paper towel rubbed with grass stains
5 drops of water
1 granola bar wrapper
A handful of dirt from the baseball field

Pile the ingredients on top of one another. Hold your medallion in one hand and hold the other hand over the pile. Chant the following spell.

Swing the bat and score a homerun!
Beginning players can have some fun!
A perfect arm to catch and throw.
Now I'm playing like a pro!

Henry leaped into action. He fished out an empty granola bar wrapper from the bottom of his backpack. Then he went outside and rubbed a paper towel on the lawn until it got grass stains.

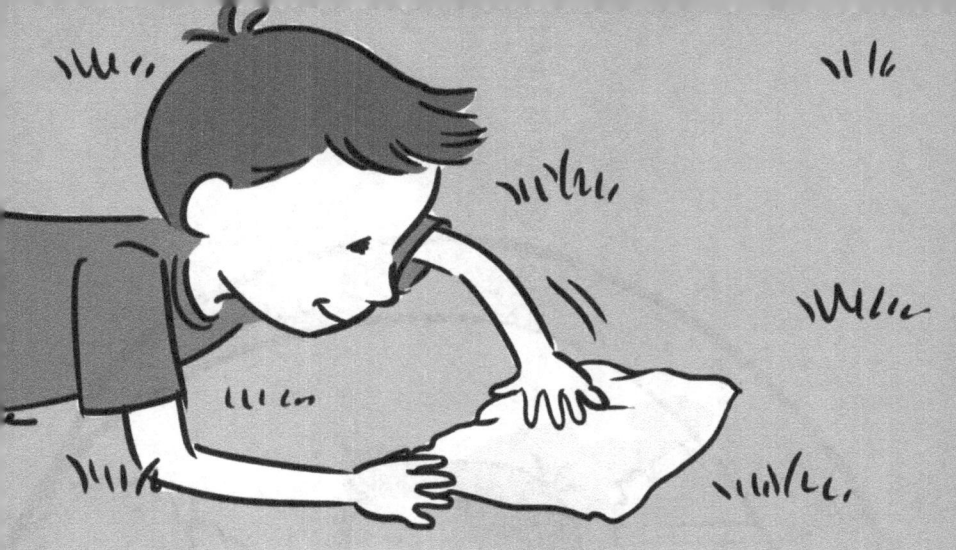

I'll get the dirt from the baseball field before the game, he told himself.

Then he rubbed his hands together. *Once I cast this spell, I'm going to be the best baseball player EVER!*

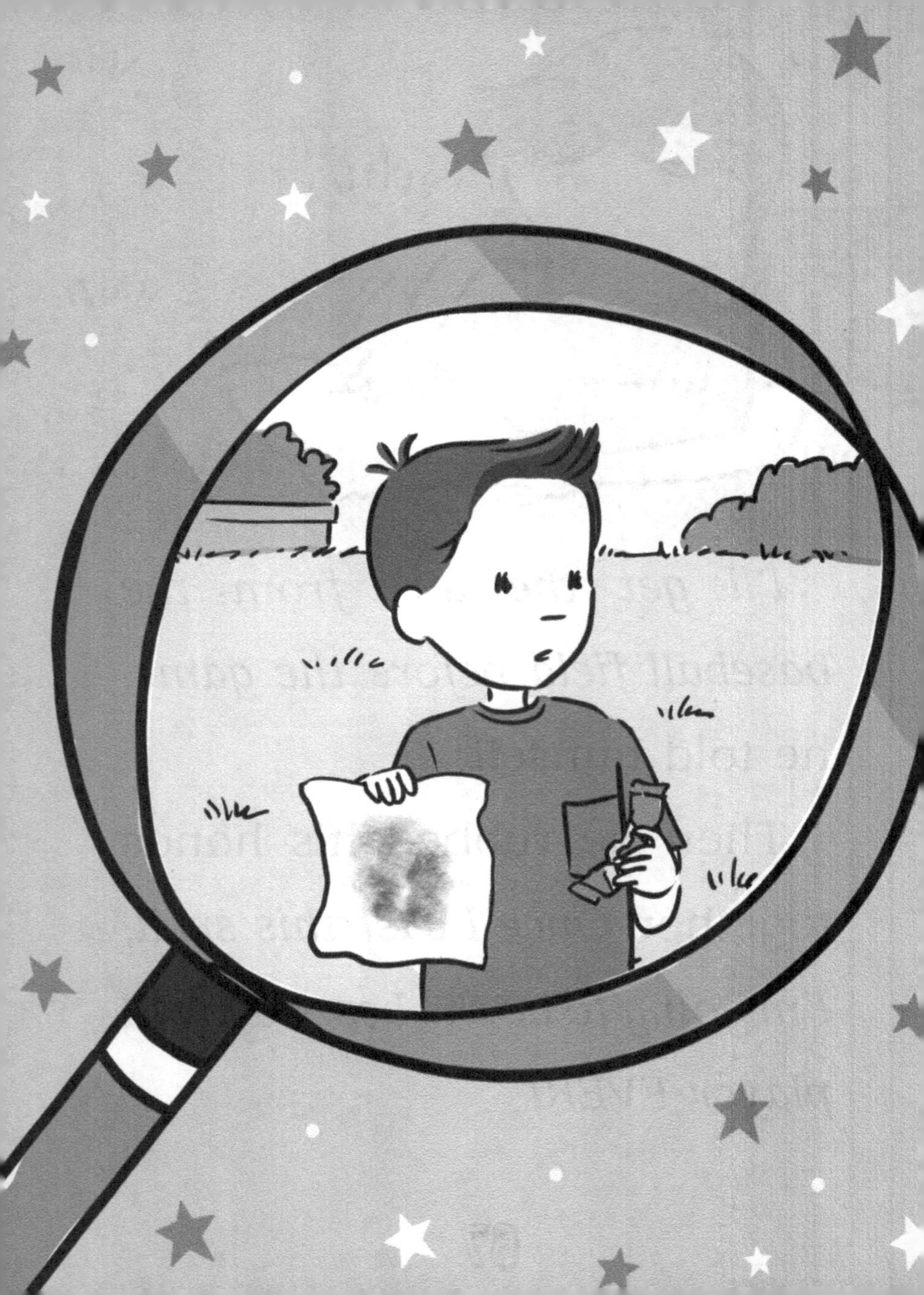

Chapter 7

TO BE A STAR

Henry got to the baseball field early on Thursday. It was time to gather some dirt from the field and cast his spell.

But there was one big problem.

Lucas had already arrived, and he was throwing a ball against the wall near the field.

Hopefully he won't even notice me, Henry thought. He stooped down and began to scoop some dirt for his spell.

"Hey, what are you doing, Heckelbeck?" asked Lucas.

Henry was so surprised that he dropped the dirt all over his sneakers.

"Oh, this?" Henry said. "This is, uh, to stop feeling nervous."

"Cool," Lucas said. He bent over and sprinkled some dirt over his sneakers too. "Thanks for showing me. I feel less nervous now."

Henry was surprised. *Lucas got nervous for baseball games? Even though he's such a good player?*

Lucas went back to practicing, so Henry quickly scooped more dirt and ran behind the stands.

He piled the dirt on the ground and added the other ingredients. Then he dripped five drops of water from his water bottle onto the pile.

Thunk! Thunk! Henry could still hear Lucas practicing his throw against the wall.

Wow, Lucas sure works hard to be the best player, he thought.

Henry stared at his spell ingredients. Did he *really* want to be the best baseball player, just as much as Lucas wanted to be?

Was it really fair to use magic?

Just then Henry heard Dudley's and Sam's voices coming closer.

Henry quickly picked up the paper towel and granola wrapper. He tossed it into the trash can before joining his teammates for warm-ups.

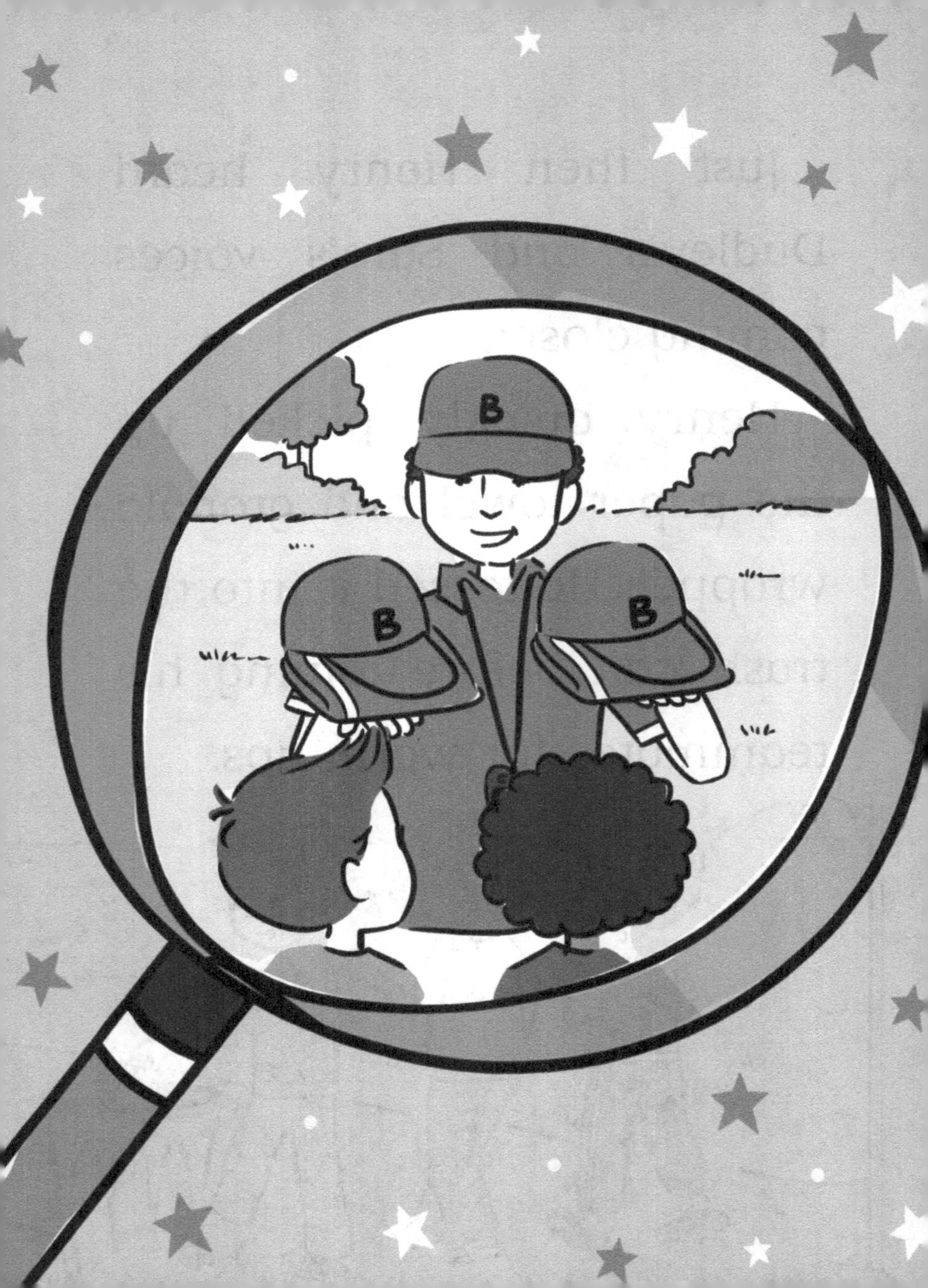

Chapter 8

LET THE GAME BEGIN

The Brewster Batters' first game of the season was against the Lightning Strikers.

Coach Hunt let Henry and Dudley borrow baseball caps and jerseys for the game.

Dudley's jersey number was 16, and Henry's was 17.

"I'll print your names on them for the next game," Coach Hunt said.

Wearing the jerseys made Henry and Dudley feel important. They walked to right field with their heads held high.

But once the game started,
Henry started getting bored.
Standing in right field was
very different from playing
catch with his friends.

Soon Henry started hoping
the ball would fly toward
him . . . just so he would have
something to do!

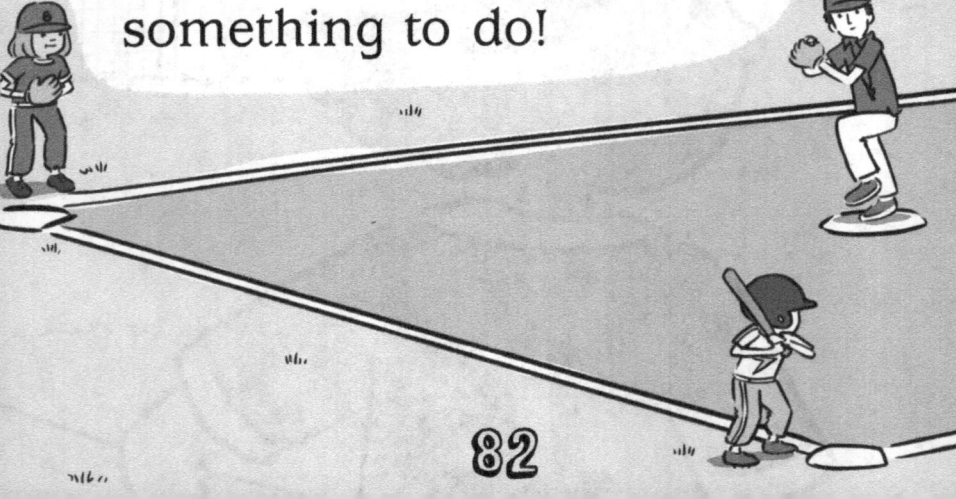

Henry and Dudley waved their hands and pointed to themselves, but the ball never came their way. Soon the Lightning Strikers had three outs.

Now it was the Brewster Batters' turn to bat. Coach Hunt lined up the players. Lucas was first and Henry was second.

Gulp.

Henry glanced at his family in the stands and spotted Max sitting next to Heidi. He quickly turned back around.

Great, he thought. *One more person to watch me strike out!*

Coach Hunt pitched the ball, and Lucas swung hard.

SMACK! As the ball soared across the field, Lucas ran all the way to third base!

The crowd clapped and cheered. Lucas held up two fingers in a *V* for victory.

Henry clapped for Lucas too, but his legs felt like jelly.

How am I supposed to follow THAT? Henry wondered. *I've never even hit the ball before!*

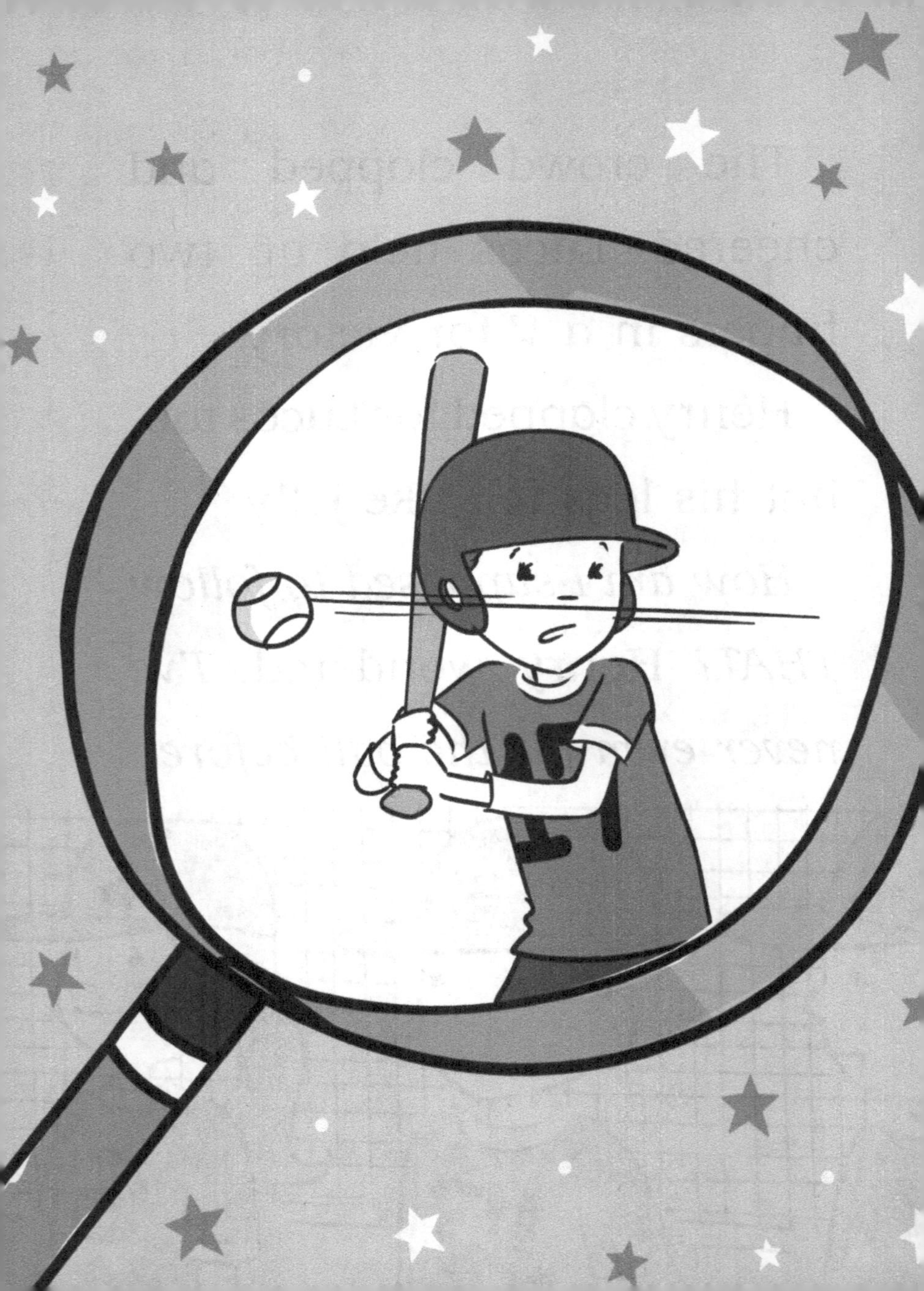

Chapter 9

HENRY IS UP!

Henry gripped the bat at home plate.

"Here we go," Coach Hunt said, pitching the ball.

ZOOM! Henry stood frozen as the ball whizzed by him.

"Strike one!" shouted the coach for the Lightning Strikers.

Henry bit his lip. He had no time to think. The next ball was coming!

This time, Henry swung. But he missed the ball completely. "Strike two!"

Henry's heart sank. He was one strike away from striking out in front of everyone on the field.

That's when Lucas called out, "Keep your eye on the ball!"

Surprised, Henry swiveled his head toward third base. Lucas gave him a thumbs-up, and Henry gave him one back. "Ready?" Coach Hunt asked.

Henry swiveled his head back and nodded. *Here goes nothing,* he thought.

Coach pitched the ball. Henry kept his eyes glued to the ball and swung.

Whack! The ball skittered across the ground between first and second base.

Henry dropped the bat and took off. But before he could get to first base, one of the Strikers caught the ball and stepped on the base.

"You're out!" the girl said.

Henry pulled his helmet
down as he ran off the field.
He didn't want anyone to see
his frown.

But for some reason, all his teammates were cheering. Dudley pointed to the scoreboard.

BREWSTER BATTERS   LIGHTNING STRIKERS

1   0

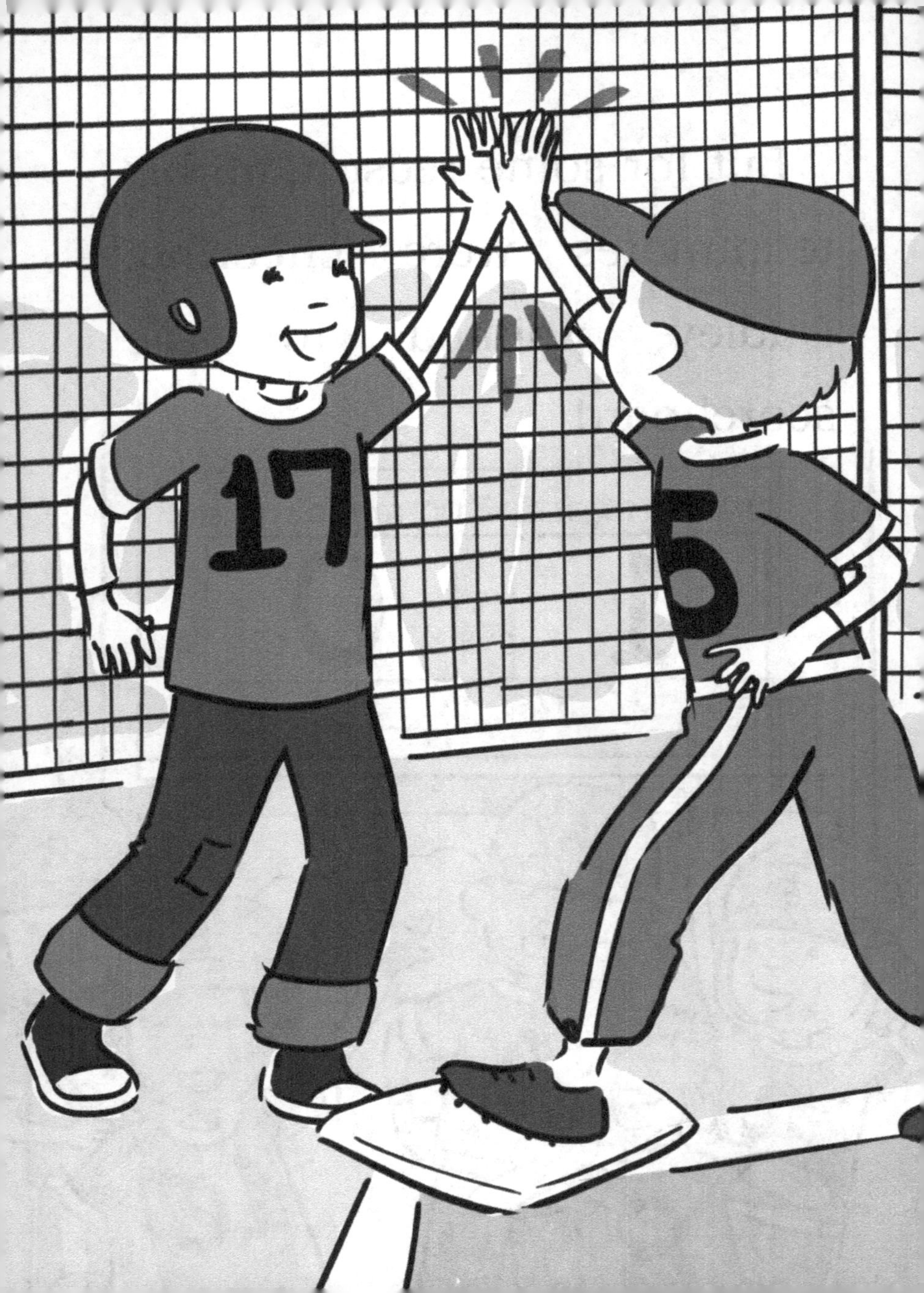
17

While Henry had been busy getting out, Lucas had run to home plate!

"Thanks, Henry!" Lucas said, high-fiving him.

"Thanks, Lucas," Henry replied, beaming. He may have gotten out, but he had also helped his team score a point.

And he hadn't needed magic to do it. He'd done it all by himself . . . with a little support from his teammates!

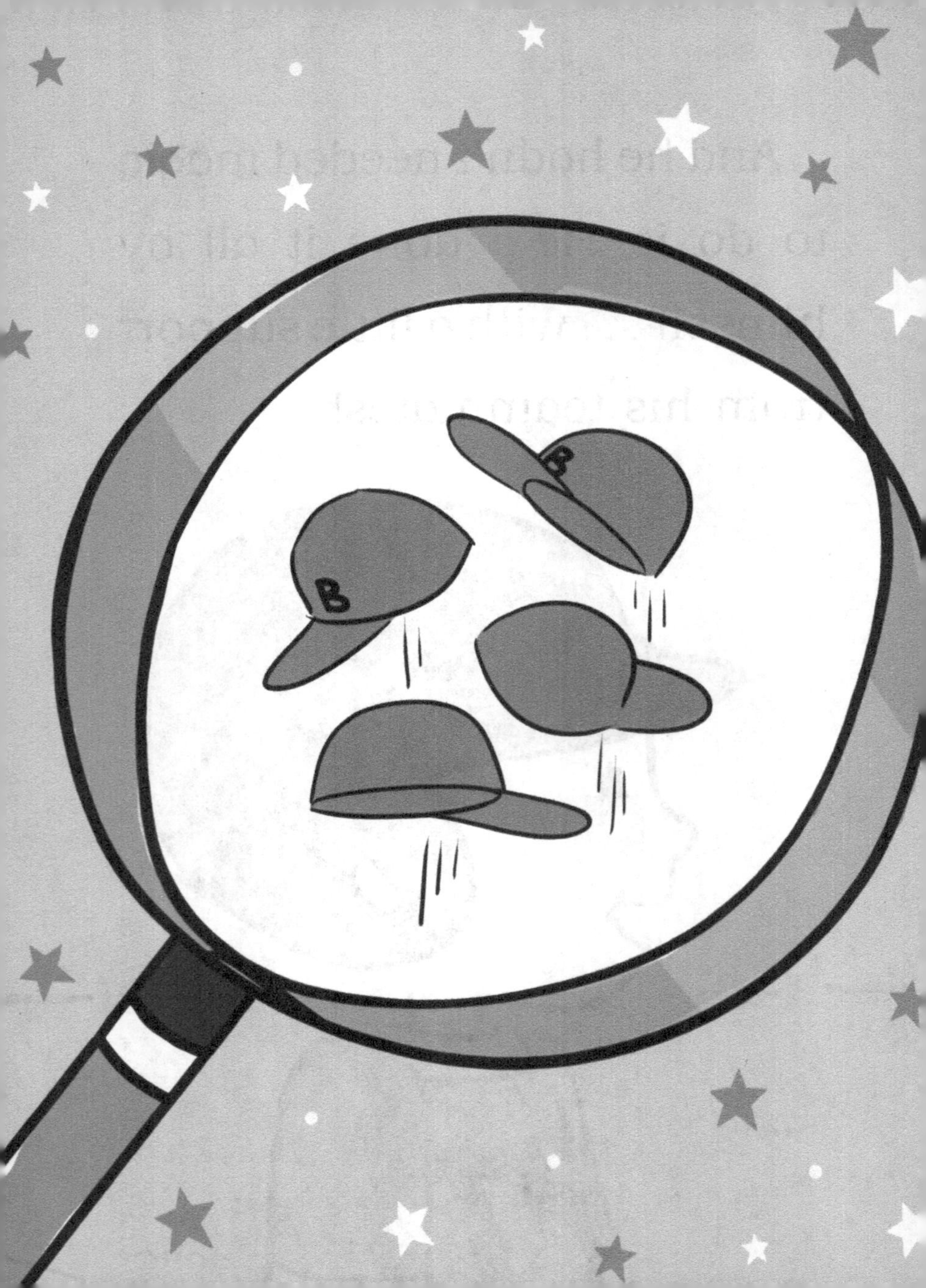
B
B

Chapter 10

BUTT WHAT?

The Brewster Batters ended up winning the game, 2 to 1.

The two teams shook hands. Then Henry and his teammates threw their caps into the air and cheered!

Henry's family, Dudley's family, and Max joined them on the field.

"Not bad, Mr. Superstar!" Heidi said, nudging her brother.

But Max frowned and said,
"You know what? I don't really
get how all the rules work in
baseball."

Henry grinned. "Well, that's funny because we don't get them very well either!"

Max laughed. Then her face got serious.

"I was worried you would get really good at baseball," she said to Henry and Dudley. "And then you would never play catch in the park with me."

Dudley shook his head. "No way! We'll *always* play catch with you!"

Henry's dad came over, waving some papers.

"Want me to give these to your coach so you can officially join the team?" he asked.

Henry and Dudley looked at
each other. They both shook
their heads.

Then they pulled off their jerseys and ran them over to Coach Hunt.

"Dudley and I decided not to join the team after all," Henry said.

"Why not?" Coach Hunt asked, raising his eyebrows.

"Well, we both like baseball," Dudley said. "But we'd rather just play it for fun."

Henry held his breath, but Coach Hunt nodded like he understood.

"I respect that," he said, giving the boys a fist bump each.

Then Henry and Dudley ran back to Max.

"Wanna play catch this weekend?" asked Henry.

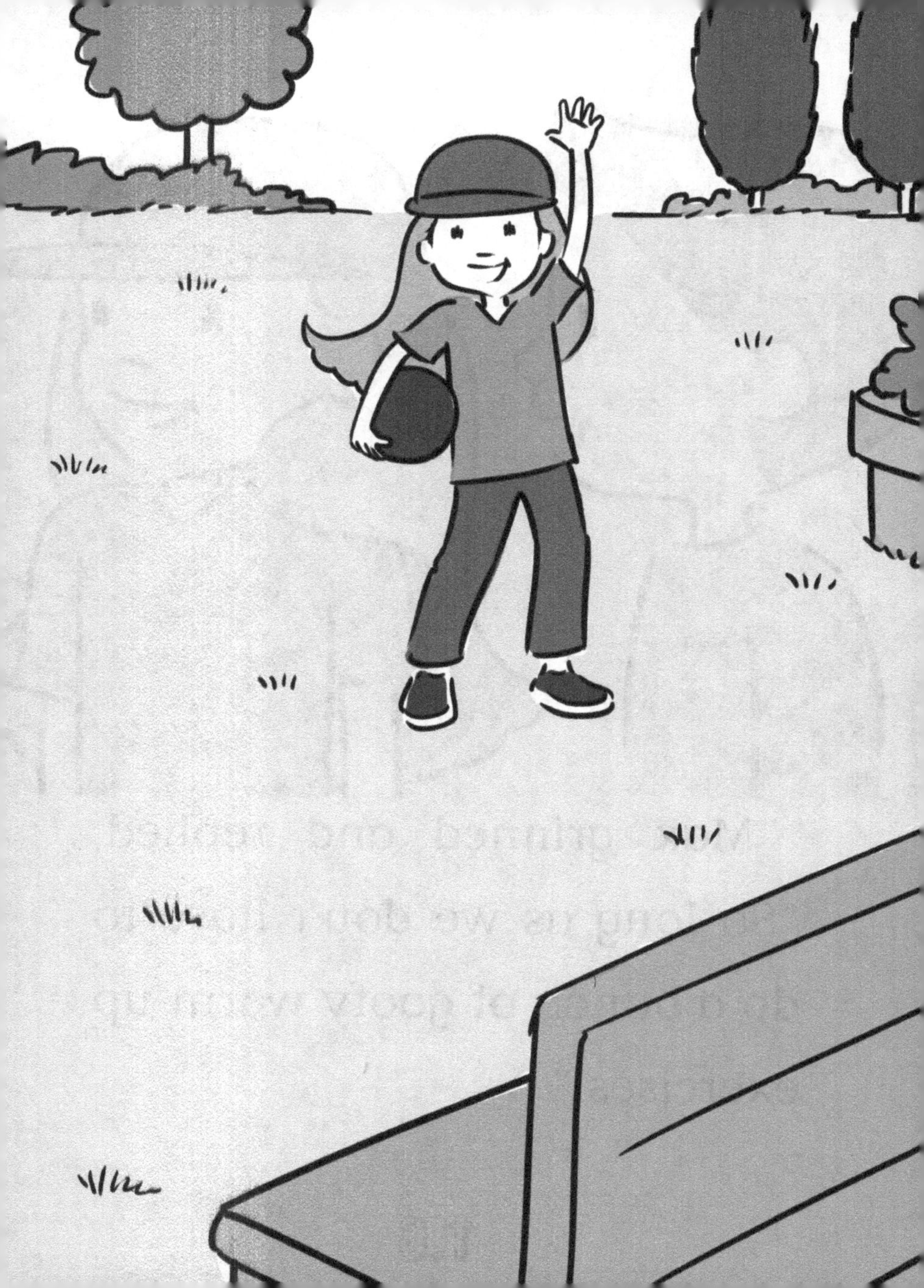

Max grinned and replied, "So long as we don't have to do a bunch of goofy warm-up exercises!"

"Not even butt-kickers?" Dudley burst out.

Heidi popped in between the three best friends. "WHAT kickers?" she asked.

Henry, Dudley, and Max looked at each other. "BUTT-kickers!" they shouted at the same time.

Then the three of them lined up and did butt-kickers all the way off the field.

Check out the next book starring

HENRY HECKELBECK

Henry's spy senses tingled.

Something is different about this morning, he thought as he sat up in bed. *But what?*

Henry looked around his room.

An excerpt from *Henry Heckelbeck and the Not-So-Dark Day*

His books stood on the bookshelves. Outside his window, clouds floated in the sky.

Everything was totally normal.

Already fully dressed, Henry jumped out of bed and flicked on the light switch. But the light didn't turn on.

Flick! Flick! Flick!

Nothing happened. So Henry

ran into the hallway and thumped down the stairs.

"The light fizzed out in my room!" he yelled.

Right outside the kitchen, Henry's spy senses tingled again.

It's too quiet, he thought.

There was no toaster dinging. No smoothie machine whirring. No music playing, or Dad humming.

An excerpt from *Henry Heckelbeck and the Not-So-Dark Day*